For Freddie with love   AM

For my big brother   S J-P

VIKING KESTREL
Published by the Penguin Group
Viking Penguin, a division of Penguin Books USA Inc.,
40 West 23rd Street, New York, New York 10010, U.S.A.
Penguin Books Ltd, 27 Wright's Lane, London W8 5TZ, England
Penguin Books Australia Ltd, Ringwood, Victoria, Australia
Penguin Books Canada Ltd, 2801 John Street, Markham,
Ontario, Canada L3R 1B4
Penguin Books (N.Z.) Ltd, 182-190 Wairau Road,
Auckland 10, New Zealand

Penguin Books Ltd, Registered Offices:
Harmondsworth, Middlesex, England

First published in Great Britain by Aurum Books for Children 1989

First American edition published in 1989

10   9   8   7   6   5   4   3   2   1

Text copyright © Angela McAllister, 1989
Illustrations copyright © Susie Jenkin-Pearce, 1989

All rights reserved

Library of Congress catalog number: 89-40247
ISBN 0–670–82991–9

Printed and bound in Italy

Snail's Birthday Problem

Story by Angela McAllister • Illustrations by Susie Jenkin-Pearce

Viking Kestrel

Snail had a problem.

All day he thought so hard about his problem that he forgot to eat.

And all night he worried so much about his problem that he couldn't sleep.

Soon his friends began to notice that he looked unhappy.

Badger tried to cheer up Snail – by bicycling backwards and juggling two bananas and a top hat.

"Chin up," said Badger. "It's your birthday soon. We'll have a party and I'll bring the balloons."

And, putting on his hat, Badger cycled home to learn some balloon tricks.

"Oh, dear," sighed Snail, "now my problem is bigger than ever!"

Rabbit tried to cheer up Snail —
by tying her ears in a bow, turning
two somersaults, a back flip and
doing the splits.

But still Snail looked worried.

"If you don't smile, your face
will stay sad forever, " said
Rabbit.

"Anyway, it's your birthday soon. We'll
have a wonderful party and I'll
bring the cake."
And Rabbit untied her ears
and skipped home to try a
new cake recipe.
"Oh, dear," sighed
Snail, "now my
problem is
bigger than
ever!"

Chicken tried to cheer up
Snail – by tying cymbals to her
knees, playing the guitar and whistling
'Here We Go Round the Mulberry Bush'.
But still Snail looked worried.

"Whatever is bothering you may never happen," said Chicken. "Remember, it's your birthday soon. We'll have a terrific party and I'll bring the decorations."
And, with a whistle, Chicken went home to make some paper lanterns.
"Oh, dear," sighed Snail, "now my problem is bigger than ever."

Mole tried to cheer up Snail –
by putting a daisy in his mouth,
wearing a grass skirt and
dancing the hula hula.
But still Snail looked worried.

"Life's too short to be sad," said Mole. "Besides, it's your birthday soon. We'll have a splendid party and I'll bring the paper hats."

And, with the daisy still in his mouth, Mole burrowed home to make some new hats.

"Oh, dear," sighed Snail, "now my problem is bigger than ever!"

Suddenly he remembered what his mother used to say: 'A problem shared is a problem halved'. Snail's problem was certainly big enough for two. So he decided to share it with Owl, who was very wise.

Snail slid slowly and sadly to Owl's house.

"Now, what, exactly, is your problem?" Owl asked.

"Well," said Snail, "soon it will be my birthday."

"I know," said Owl, knowingly. "You must have a party and invite all your friends."

"But THAT IS THE PROBLEM!" sighed Snail.

"You see, Badger had a
birthday party at his house
and, although it was a little
smelly there and Mole caught
a cold from the damp leaves,
we all had a wonderful time..."

" . . . Rabbit had a birthday party at her house and, although Chicken got lost in the warren, we all had a wonderful time . . ."

" . . . and Chicken had a birthday party at her house and, although it was very feathery there, and Badger sneezed until his glasses flew off, we all had a wonderful time...

" . . . Mole had a birthday
party at his house and, although
it was a little dark in there
and Rabbit bumped her nose,
we all had a wonderful time.

Now it is my turn to have a
birthday party and everyone is
looking forward to it . . . but . . .
I CAN'T INVITE ANYONE
INTO MY HOUSE!"

"Ah ha!" said Owl. "We shall have to look in my Big Book of Problems." She turned to the page marked 'P' for 'Parties'. Snail waited and waited. At last Owl smiled wisely. "The solution is to have a Garden Party!" "But . . . I don't have a garden!" Snail sighed.

"Oh, yes, you do. You take your house
wherever you go, so the whole world
is your garden!" said Owl. And she
sat down, quite exhausted.

Snail smiled. His problem
was solved. "The whole
world is my garden!
EVERYONE can
come to my
party!"

On the day of the party, Badger brought balloons. Rabbit brought a three tier lettuce cake. Mole brought sparkly crowns. And Chicken brought paper lanterns.

No one got a cold or got lost, bumped his nose or broke his glasses.

Last to arrive was Owl with a tiny present. "Happy birthday, Snail," she said with a wink.

Snail carefully unwrapped the parcel and found a small doorma with the word WELCOME on it.

"Put that outside your shell," said Owl, "and friends will visit you wherever you go!"

Snail was so pleased that he danced a wriggly jig, singing 'Happy Birthday to Me!'